Isla OF ADVENTURE

THE CRITTER CAFÉ

by Dela Costa   illustrated by Ana Sebastián

LITTLE SIMON

New York London Toronto Sydney New Delhi

LITTLE SIMON
An imprint of Simon & Schuster Children's Publishing Division
1230 Avenue of the Americas, New York, New York 10020
First Little Simon hardcover edition September 2023
Copyright © 2023 by Simon & Schuster, Inc.
All rights reserved, including the right of reproduction in whole or in part in any form.
LITTLE SIMON is a registered trademark of Simon & Schuster, Inc., and associated colophon is a trademark of Simon & Schuster, Inc. For information about special discounts for bulk purchases, please contact Simon & Schuster Special Sales at 1-866-506-1949 or business@simonandschuster.com.
The Simon & Schuster Speakers Bureau can bring authors to your live event. For more information or to book an event contact the Simon & Schuster Speakers Bureau at 1-866-248-3049 or visit our website at www.simonspeakers.com.
Series designed by Laura Roode.
Book designed by Laura Roode. The text of this book was set in Congenial.
Manufactured in the United States of America 0823 LAK
2 4 6 8 10 9 7 5 3 1
Cataloging-in-Publication Data is available for this title from the Library of Congress.
ISBN 978-1-6659-3970-6 (hc)
ISBN 978-1-6659-3969-0 (pbk)
ISBN 978-1-6659-3971-3 (ebook)

Contents

TROUBLE IN BERRY LAND

◆◆◆◆◆◆◆◆◆◆◆◆◆◆

The sweet, mouthwatering scent of cinnamon muffins wrapped around Isla Verde.

She eagerly watched the muffins slowly rise through the oven door.

Fitz, Isla's gecko best friend, sighed happily as he sat on her shoulder. Just as Isla loved everything about her home in Sol, Fitz loved everything to do with food. Especially Abuela's baking. So it was lucky Isla lived right next door to her grandparents!

"This oven is my new best friend," Fitz said dreamily. "Wow . . . look how it bakes."

Isla laughed. "Are you replacing me with an oven?"

"Jeez, can you blame me? This thing is a baking machine," Fitz joked. "And it smells a-ma-zing."

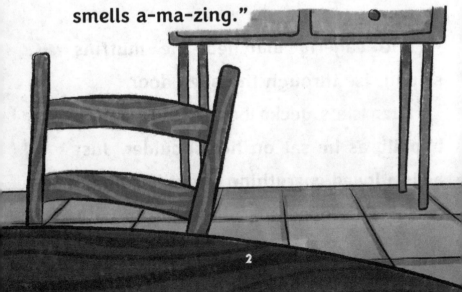

"Now you're just saying I'm stinky."
Isla lifted a hair curl and sniffed. "Maybe
my new shampoo isn't strong enough.
The rain forest frogs made it from river
water."

Fitz stuck his tongue out. "*That*
explains it!"

From squeaky clean counters to the latest blender model, everything in Abuela's kitchen was the best of the best. She was a cookbook writer, so it made sense she had an oven even a gecko loved.

It was also no wonder Abuela had won the annual Sol Bake Off so many times. Abuelo had even built a special shelf to hold the five glittering Golden Spoon trophies.

Click!

Broken out of her sugary trance, Isla turned to see her grandparents coming in from the backyard.

"Hola, hola!" Abuela said. She undid the big bow on her apron, slipped her apron off, and folded it over a chair.

Like Mama, Abuela could often be found wearing a stained apron. Mama's was usually covered with soil and Abuela's with flour.

"The berries for tomorrow are here!" Fitz cheered. "Come on!"

Isla stood up and skipped to the table.

"How was it? Did you pick enough raspberries? Did you?" she asked in a rush. When she was excited, Isla spoke as quickly as a hummingbird flew. "I just *know* you'll win the Golden Spoon again, Abuela!"

Her grandparents shared a look that made Isla pause. It was the kind of expression Fitz had when he ran out of banana slices to eat. Not very good.

"We didn't have much luck this time," Abuelo said. He pushed the basket across the table. "See?"

Isla peered inside to see just a few dried-up berries. They definitely weren't enough to whip up the raspberry scones Abuela planned to bake.

"These don't look berry-licious." Fitz pouted. "Not even *I* would eat them, and I eat everything."

"Oh no!" Isla groaned. "But the berry bushes were filled yesterday."

"Maybe someone ate a big breakfast," Abuela joked, winking at Fitz.

"It wasn't me this time." Fitz chuckled nervously. Sometimes, he forgot only Isla could speak to and understand animals.

"I can stop by the marketplace," Isla offered. "The raspberries won't be from the backyard, but they'll still be from Sol."

"That would be nice of you, Isla." Abuelo's eyes wrinkled as he smiled. "Up for an adventure?"

She was Isla Verde—adventure *called* to her!

"Of course. I'll be back!" she shouted, rushing out the door and strapping on her bike helmet.

Inside the bike basket, Fitz spun in happy circles. "Finally, an adventure I can really sink my teeth into!"

SOMETHING ODD

◆◆◆◆◆◆◆◆◆◆◆◆◆

The Sol marketplace was a quick bike ride from Isla's neighborhood.

She was no stranger to the hardworking street vendors, happy customers, and talented musicians. Not to mention, Isla's ability to speak to animals came in handy during market visits. They always helped her find the best deals.

Isla zoomed through and parked outside the grocery store.

Fitz crawled up her arm. "Jeez, what a nice day. Pretty quiet, too."

At first glance, everything looked to be business as usual.

But usually a tortoise needed help moving out of the road. Sometimes a chatty iguana had gossip to share from all corners of Sol. If they were really unlucky, a singing seagull showed up to squawk loudly.

Isla frowned. "Is there something odd about this place today?"

Fitz pointed at a fruit stand nearby. "I'm so glad you mentioned it! Can you believe no one sells dragon fruit anymore?"

Isla laughed. "Remember when you thought it came from actual dragons?"

Fitz blushed at the memory. "Hey! I was just a hatchling back then. . . ."

A dragon fruit's pink, scaly skin *did* make the fruit look magical. But that wasn't what Isla meant. Besides Fitz, there were no animals in sight. Where were her friends?

"No, no, no. I know what you're thinking!" Fitz said accusingly.

Isla raised her eyebrows. "Oh, you can read minds now?"

"You're thinking about forgetting this fun plan and doing something else," Fitz said. "This is supposed to be a delicious, I mean, an *easy* mission."

"Okay, okay," Isla said. "First, we find the fruit."

Fitz's tail wagged excitedly. "Woo-hoo! Then we go straight home to eat the fruit—I mean, *bake* with the fruit."

The grocery doors slid open as Fitz led the way inside. They walked toward a sign that read FRUITS & VEGGIES. But when they arrived, both Isla and Fitz stopped midstep. The fruit crates were completely empty.

THE CASE OF THE MISSING BERRIES

◇◇◇◇◇◇◇◇◇◇◇◇◇◇

"Where are the raspberries?" Isla ran from crate to empty crate. "Where are *any* of the berries?"

Fitz hopped into a crate with nothing but bare grapevines. He spun in circles. "No oranges or pears in sight. What about the blueberries? Even the mangoes are gone! Oh, mangoes . . . I never really knew you!"

"I'm sure there's a good explanation," Isla said.

At least, I hope there is, she thought nervously. *This is a berry wasteland.*

"*Hola*, Isla!" a voice said. "Find any good leftovers?"

It was Mr. Martin, the store manager. He wore a vest and held a clipboard. His glasses sat on the tip of his nose.

"Leftovers?" Isla squeaked. "You mean, everything's sold out?"

A few workers started to fold empty cartons. Fitz moved to Isla's shoulder as the crates were removed too.

Mr. Martin nodded. "Just this morning, Mrs. Rosa bought three bushels of strawberries. Even the bananas sold out. Ten whole crates gone in seconds! The Sol Bake Off boosts sales!"

"I guess no one wants to bake with veggies," Isla muttered.

"Hey, there's an idea!" Mr. Martin exclaimed. "Instead of fruits, try using some greens."

They turned to look at the overflowing crates of lettuce, tomatoes, carrots, spinach, and other not-so-sweet veggies.

"Tomato cupcakes? Spinach donuts?" Fitz swayed dizzily. "I'm just not that kind of gecko."

Isla slumped.

"*Lo siento*, kiddo. I'm sorry," Mr. Martin said. "But don't you worry! I'm already placing a huge order. See?"

He turned over the clipboard. Sure enough, he'd marked everything they needed, and more.

"Amazing!" Isla said. "When should I come back?"

"Not until tomorrow afternoon," Mr. Martin said, then frowned. "Which is *after* the Bake Off."

"We're doomed!" Fitz cried.

Isla looked at the empty crates nervously.

Mr. Martin smiled encouragingly. "You Verdes are champs! If anyone can figure it out, it's you guys."

CHAPTER 4

LONGTAIL

◆◆◆◆◆◆◆◆◆◆◆◆◆◆

"Think, gecko, think!" Fitz paced back and forth on the sidewalk.

Isla sat on the curb outside the grocery store. She watched as vendors closed up shop. They had run out of fruits to sell too.

"You Verdes are champs," Mr. Martin had said. Right now, though, Isla wasn't feeling like one.

"Why can't my secret power be growing fruits?" She sighed.

Fitz sat beside Isla. "Hey, it might be worth a try."

Isla could tell Fitz was trying to make her feel better. She squeezed her eyes shut and wiggled her fingers out in front of her. She imagined a pile of raspberries appearing before them. But nothing happened.

Fitz nudged her knee. "Maybe you just need an extra friendship boost."

Together, they wiggled their fingers and laughed. Maybe that hadn't worked, but shared laughter was a better result.

"*Squeak!*" came a sudden sound.

"Did you say something?" Isla and Fitz asked at the same time.

A small, round-eared mouse skittered around the legs of a fruit cart. Isla noticed the mouse carried a bundle made of wrapped leaves on his back. Inside it, something gleamed.

She whispered, "I think our magic fingers worked."

The mouse began muttering to himself. "That's the last of them—*squeak*! Longtail has done a great job!"

"The last of what?" Fitz asked. "And who's Longtail?"

The mouse's twitching nose froze as he realized he wasn't alone. Looking up slowly, he came face-to-face with a curious Isla and Fitz. "Oh my!" he said. "Longtail didn't see you there. But, um, Longtail must return . . . to the Critter Café . . . now."

"Great to meet you, Longtail." Isla smiled. "What's the Critter Café?"

"And why is your name Longtail when your tail is short?" Fitz asked suspiciously.

"Fitz!" Isla chided. "You can't just ask critters that."

The mouse tucked down his tail and backed away. "Oh no . . . questions. Longtail can't keep secrets—*squeak*!"

The mouse dashed off so quickly that his leaf bundle came unwrapped. A few red glistening objects fell out.

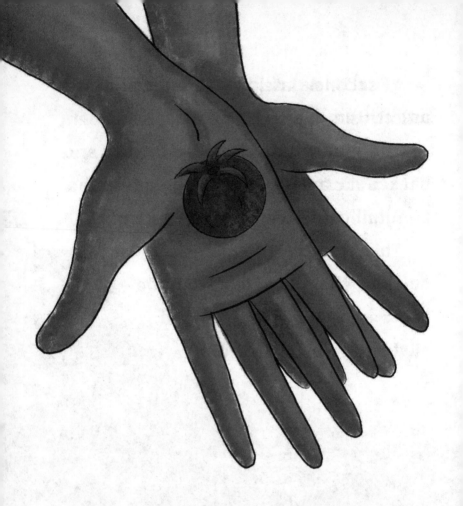

Fitz's eyes widened. "Is that what I think it is?"

"Berries," Isla whispered, bending down to pick them up. "*Big* berries."

A second later, they sprang into action. Isla placed Fitz on her shoulder, then ran after Longtail. She'd never run after a mouse before, but there was a first time for everything.

It was hard to keep track of a tiny mouse as he weaved in between shoppers.

"Excuse me!" Isla tried her best to not bump into shopping bags. "Oops, *perdon*. Pardon me!"

A line of jolly musicians cut through the chase, causing her to lose sight of Longtail.

Then someone shouted, "*RATÓN! MOUSE!*"

"Gotcha!" Isla said, running in the direction of the screams.

Longtail was trapped between two spooked kids. Seeing that he'd been found, he crawled over the screaming boy's shoes and dashed off.

"Come back, Longtail!" Fitz shouted. "How will I try Abuela's delicious scones if she can't bake them?"

Isla ran out of the marketplace and chased Longtail down a dirt path. The grass became taller. She zigzagged between wildflowers.

"Watch out!" Fitz tugged on one of Isla's curls and pointed ahead. "Crawling snails on the path!"

Isla hopped over the cluster of slow garden snails, then ducked underneath low tree branches. It wasn't long before Longtail completely disappeared.

Isla stopped to catch her breath. "I think we lost him."

CHAPTER 5

INTRUDER
ALERT!

◊◊◊◊◊◊◊◊◊◊◊◊◊

Wild grass tickled Isla's legs as she walked through a large meadow. Flowering trees were scattered throughout, leaving behind a sweet smell.

Fitz moved to the top of Isla's head for a better look. "We're in the tree grove. Trees with flowers usually mean there should be fruit."

He was right. But as Isla walked

from tree to tree, she didn't see a single hanging orange or mango.

"There really is something odd at play here," she said. "And I don't think it's critters having a big breakfast."

Fitz threw his hands up. "Please, great island of Sol. Help us! Give us a sign!"

"*Squeak!*" came the response.

"Um, since when can you speak to the island?" Isla asked, surprised.

"I'm more powerful than I realized," Fitz said. "Wait, no—there's Longtail!"

The mouse was a few feet away, climbing over a low stone wall.

"Great eye, Fitz," Isla whispered. She high-fived her best friend.

45

Just as Longtail hopped to the other side, Isla reached the wall. But a loud, angry voice stopped her cold.

"Hey, hey, hey! What do you MEAN you dropped ALL the berries?" the voice boomed.

Isla hid behind a nearby tree.

"S-sorry," Longtail replied. "A human and a gecko were chasing me, and—"

"HUMANS and GECKOS don't just hang out!" the angry voice interrupted. "HOW am I supposed to cook MY dish now?!"

Isla and Fitz shared a funny look. Humans and geckos *totally* hung out.

"*Squeak*—I'll go find more!" Longtail said. The sound of crunching leaves let Isla know he scurried off again.

"You're not thinking of going back there, are you?" Fitz asked nervously.

"I have to!" Isla replied. "They could have the answer to our *berry* serious problem."

Fitz sighed. "Yeah, I knew you'd say something like that."

Isla slowly stepped out from behind the tree and peeked over the stone wall. The sight before her was a total surprise.

A group of animals was spread out
with dozens of food-packed dishes.

Iguanas sliced mangoes with their long nails, then placed the slices on tree bark. Monkeys peeled bananas and smashed them into bowls made of giant leaves. Toucans plucked berries from branches, then dropped them into coconut shells. Bees buzzed and dragged honey from a hive.

"Are you seeing this?" Isla rubbed her eyes, then looked again.

Fitz's mouth dropped open. "If this is a dream, *please* don't wake me up."

"Who runs this thing?" Isla wondered.

A small, furry body suddenly hopped onto the stone wall. Isla and Fitz jumped back in surprise.

"WHO runs this THING?" Though the critter was tiny, his voice was mighty. "A CHEF who doesn't like INTRUDERS, that's who!"

THE CRITTER CAFÉ!

◆◇◆◇◆◇◆◇◆◇◆◇◆

Six pairs of surprised eyes turned to stare.

Fitz pulled down a large leaf to hide behind. "Gecko out!"

Isla studied the critter. *Big round eyes, short body, pointy ears, and a tail that curls at the bottom. This reminds me of a critter I read about in a book. . . .*

Isla gasped, remembering a book

about far-away tree-dwellers. "You're a mouse lemur, aren't you? I've read all about you! Fitz, are you seeing this? A mouse lemur . . . in *Sol*!"

"I don't want to see *or* be seen," Fitz replied.

The mouse lemur snatched away Fitz's leaf and glared. "INTRUDERS may call me CHEF Plum."

"Do you like plums?" Fitz asked.

"Absolutely . . . NOT," Chef Plum replied. "Have you come to steal my recipes?"

Isla waved her hands. "Not at all!"

"Oh, silly lemur," said a familiar
iguana. "That's our dear human friend,
Isla."

Mia, one of Isla's chattier friends,
waved. The rest of the animals did too.

"I was wondering where you were!"
Isla said. "I didn't know you were part
of this um . . . restaurant?"

"I'm surprised she didn't tell us about it before," Fitz said. "She's always talking our ears off!"

Mia crawled up the wall and pulled Fitz into a tight hug. "Darling gecko! Are you still upset I told everyone about the time you slipped on a banana peel?"

"The Critter Café isn't a restaurant," explained a monkey. "It's a cooking club."

A toucan flew over and landed on Isla's head. "We gather once a year. Humans have the Bake Off, and we have this!"

So, this is where all the fruit has gone!
Isla realized.

Humans emptied the marketplace, and the island gave the animals all the fruit they needed.

Chef Plum suddenly shushed everyone. "WAIT a MOMENT. You're Isla . . . VERDE?"

"Yup!" Isla said. "This cute gecko is Fitz, by the way. Sol Adventurers, at your service."

"One moment!" Chef Plum climbed up a tree and returned with a crumpled drawing. It looked like the Golden Spoon. "Aren't you the winner of THIS trophy?"

"Oh, *that*?" Isla waved a hand. "I just help out."

"And maybe you could help us out," Fitz said. "Abuela can't enter this year without raspberries, and I see plenty over there."

A toucan quickly covered a pile of berries with a wing. "Uh, yeah, there's just one teeny-tiny problem. We need them to enter the contest."

Isla frowned. "Contest?"

"Isla Verde," Chef Plum said, squeezing the drawing. "It is our GREATEST dream to enter the Sol Bake Off. Won't you consider tasting and using one of OUR dishes?"

TASTE–TESTER FITZ

◆◆◆◆◆◆◆◆◆◆◆◆◆

Chef Plum took Isla's hand and ushered her closer to the many, many Critter Café dishes.

There were bowls of fruit, a Worms-N-Dirt smoothie, puddings, and a few other things Isla couldn't name. Fitz looked at everything with heart eyes.

"Hmm, I have an idea," Isla said. "What if Fitz tried the dishes instead?

He's a more, ah, adventurous eater."

Fitz wiped away a happy tear. "This is my dream job."

"WONDERFUL!" Chef Plum said. His big eyes turned to the rest of the animals. "CRITTER CAFÉ! Prepare your meals!"

First, the toucans stepped up. One of the beautiful birds used her wing to push forward a coconut bowl filled with berries.

"These berries are the sweetest in all of Sol, straight from Abuela Verde's backyard," she said. "Glazed with honey and sprinkled with wild dandelions!"

"You could've asked Abuela's permission, you know." Fitz plopped a few berries into his mouth. "She always lets ME eat them. Delicious, as always!"

Next, the monkeys brought leaf bowls of smashed bananas. A delicate brown seasoning was sprinkled on top.

Fitz dipped a finger and tried it. "Ooh. Is this chocolate powder?"

A monkey lifted his grass-covered foot. "It's dirt! I made this with my own feet."

Fitz looked like he was going to be sick. "Oh . . . nice?"

Finally, Mia used her tail to drag Fitz toward the iguana's mango board. "Just for you, dear gecko," she said. "Cold, fresh, and colorful!"

In a blink of an eye, Fitz ate most of the mango in one gulp. "So . . . tasty . . . I can't . . . move."

He was so full, Isla couldn't help but laugh. "So? Which is your favorite?"

The animals leaned in as Fitz thought carefully.

"Hmm. . . . It's hard to say," he said, rubbing his belly. "The honey from the mango is very tasty. Bananas are always a good way to go . . . without the dirt. And mixed berries—"

Chef Plum snapped his fingers. "Of course! We should make a mixed-berry compote drizzled with honey!"

Isla blinked in surprise. "A what now?"

"Compote is blended fruit with a bit of sugar," Fitz explained. "You can make it warm or cold."

An idea sparked in Isla's mind. "You know . . . if we don't have enough berries for Abuela's scones and your dish . . . maybe we could share a compote?" she asked hopefully.

Chef Plum staggered backward.

"Whoa, there!" A toucan spread her wings to hold him up.

"Do you . . . do you MEAN it?" Chef Plum asked, touched. "You would HONOR the Critter Café by using OUR compote for Abuela Verde's crumbly, buttery scones?"

Isla stuck out her hand. "Shake on it?"

Chef Plum didn't hesitate to accept. "Let's *BAKE* it happen!"

CHAPTER 8

COMPOSING COMPOTE

◆◆◆◆◆◆◆◆◆◆◆◆◆

Making food at Abuela's house was always a great time. But with the Critter Café? It was a blast!

"Let's set up some ground rules," Isla said.

"Ah, yes, GROUND RULES!" Chef Plum echoed. "A STRONG foundation. Important for ALL desserts, so nothing crumbles!"

Isla lifted a finger. "First, we need gloves. It's important to keep our hands clean while touching food."

"GLOVES!" Chef Plum repeated.

"Leave that to us," the monkeys said. They climbed up a tree and disappeared into the canopy.

"Should we use clean water to clean the fruits?" Fitz asked. "No offense, but I don't think humans should eat dirt."

A round blue bird took a sip of the Worms-N-Dirt smoothie. *"Hmph!* More for me."

"WATER." Chef Plum's tail pointed at the toucans.

They flew into the air in a colorful swirl. "Coming right up!"

Finally, Isla looked through the remaining materials. The coconut shells were sparkling clean, but maybe they needed spoons to stir with instead of sticks. They were, after all, covered with crawling ants.

She tapped her chin. "Mia, do you think—?"

"I already know what you're going to say," Mia interrupted, hurrying away. "I know *everything*, dearest. Iguanas, come!"

"MARVELOUS!" Chef Plum cried. "There's nothing better than a kitchen that works together."

In no time the monkeys returned with gloves. Water dripped from the air as the toucans used their talons to lower buckets of clean water. The iguanas returned too with mixing spoons that looked suspiciously like Abuela's.

"Are we ready to make some compote, Critter Café?" Isla asked, holding a spoon in the air.

"YES!" the Critter Café responded.

"Let us BEGIN!" Chef Plum shouted.

Fitz and the iguanas dunked the remaining berries into the water. Wearing gloves, Isla listened to the monkeys as they told her how to best wash the berries.

"It's all about being gentle," a monkey said. "You don't want to squish them."

After the berries were washed, Isla moved them to a coconut bowl. When the bowl was filled, she wiped her brow and turned to Chef Plum.

"Alright," Isla said. "It's all up to you now, Chef!"

The mouse lemur began to mash the berries with the stirring spoon. He stirred and mashed until just a few chunks of fruit were left. The honeybees returned to drizzle honey on top.

"Time to taste-test,"
Chef Plum said. "Why
don't we ALL give it a try?"

Using the spoon, Isla scooped up
enough for everyone to dip a finger
into.

Mia swung Fitz around in circles.
"This is MARVELOUS! I must
serve it at my next
party."
"Put me down!"
Fitz cried. "I need
one—more—taste!"

Chef Plum gave Isla a thumbs-up, and the Critter Café gasped.

"He's never given a thumbs-up," a monkey whispered.

"Looks like we've got a winner on our hands," Isla said.

She couldn't wait for tomorrow.

CHAPTER 9

AND THE WINNER IS . . .

◆◆◆◆◆◆◆◆◆◆◆◆◆

The big day finally arrived.

Bright and early, Abuelo drove them to the marketplace.

"I'm so excited!" Isla squealed, unable to stay still in the back. "Abuela, how do you feel? I am going to burst into a ton of tiny little Islas! Right, Fitz?"

Fitz yawned on her lap. "It's too early to feel anything."

Abuela turned in the passenger seat. "I still can't believe you found someone to share this wonderful compote with us. Remind me, what was their name?"

"Um, a friend!" Isla quickly said. "Annie . . . Malls."

Fitz snorted. "Annie Malls, as in animals? Clever!"

Abuelo turned into the marketplace parking lot, where others had already arrived.

Every year, the space was cleared for the Bake Off. Stalls were pushed to the side to make room for a judge's booth. Long tables were set up for contestants to place their delicious entries.

95

Stepping outside, Isla peeked at what the others carried. She saw cakes, tarts, flans, puddings; the smells were amazing. Fitz sighed. "I love living in Sol."

Isla looked around to see if she recognized any animal friends. "I don't see Chef Plum, Mia, or any of the other critters yet. Do you?"

"Nope, nope, and nope," Fitz replied.
"Maybe they're running late."

Abuela handed Isla the covered serving dish holding her scones. "Why don't you place this on the table while I go fill out our entry card? Oh, and let me know if you see Annie Malls."

"I'm sure they're around somewhere," Isla replied.

Isla placed Abuela's dish beside a tray of mega-pink strawberry cupcakes. Abuela filled out her entry card.

"Good luck!" Isla said, hugging Abuela.

"*Gracias*—
thank you, Isla,"
Abuela replied.

Isla recognized Miss Honey, Miss Flor, and Mr. Martin as the judging began.

"Welcome, everyone!" Miss Honey announced. "As you all know, we will taste everyone's dishes and pick the top three. We do not know which entry belongs to whom as we're tasting. That way, it's a surprise for everyone. Dishes will be judged on taste and creativity. Let's begin!"

The crowd gathered eagerly. Isla, Abuelo, Abuela, and Fitz huddled together as the judges sampled each dish.

"This is taking forever!" Fitz groaned. "If it were me, I would've been done tasting by now!"

Isla giggled. "Waiting *is* the hardest part."

Finally, the judges stood in the center of the marketplace. They each held an envelope.

Miss Honey stepped up first. She slipped out a card and read it out loud. "In third place is . . . Lookin' Pine Pineapple Ice Cream!"

The Alvarez family accepted a bronze trophy, waving as everyone clapped.

"I can't wait to taste that later!" Fitz said.

Next, it was Miss Flor's turn. She opened her envelope and turned it over for everyone to see. "Second place is taken by . . . Pinkin' Delicious Strawberry Cupcakes! Would you just look at how pink they are!"

Isla cheered as her friend and neighbor, Tora Rosa, stepped forward and bowed.

Finally, Mr. Martin came forward to announce the winner of this year's first-place trophy. With the sun brightly shining on it, the Golden Spoon was extra shiny.

Isla squeezed her Abuela's hand.

"My stomach hurts, and it's not from all the food!" Fitz whispered.

"The time has come to announce the first-place winner," Mr. Martin said. "This year's Sol Bake Off champion is . . . the Berry Kind Compote!"

The marketplace burst with cheers and applause.

AN UNEXPECTED SURPRISE

◊◊◊◊◊◊◊◊◊◊◊◊◊

"Huh?" Isla looked at Abuela. "Do they mean your dish, Abuela? But you had scones."

"The *scones* are mine," Abuela said. "But thanks to your friend's compote, I was able to enter a complete dish."

"Annie was a great help," Abuelo agreed. "So they deserve the trophy this year."

"Is the winner here?" Mr. Martin asked. "Please step forward to accept the Golden Spoon."

"What now?" Fitz asked.

Isla couldn't see the Critter Café and it's not like they could come forward. Taking a deep breath, she stepped up.

"Um, hi! I'll be accepting on behalf of Annie Malls . . . they're a little shy. But a great chef!"

Mr. Martin handed over the trophy. "You're a great friend, Isla. Cheers to the new Sol Bake Off champion! Now it's time for everyone to try the food. Enjoy!"

"Oh, I will!" Fitz said, dashing away to the tables.

Later that night, Isla was journaling about her day when a sound made her stop.

Tap! Tap! Tap!

Fitz climbed up the windowsill and brightened. "It's the Critter Café!"

Isla pulled open the window. The Critter Café spilled into her bedroom loudly, landing on her bed or banging into her dresser. They all spoke at once, making it hard to understand what anyone was saying.

"Shh!" Fitz hissed. "You're causing a ruckus!"

"Oh, but we're so GRATEFUL!" Chef Plum cried out, leaving little footprints on Isla's journal. "OUR compote helped Abuela WIN!"

Isla was surprised. "Were you there the whole time?"

"Why, of course!" Mia said, looking at herself in Isla's mirror. "We were watching from your car. Oh, I hope Abuelo doesn't mind that I left a tiny little scratch on the top."

"Uh . . . ," Isla said.

"I didn't know Abuela's real name was Annie Malls," a toucan said. "I just thought it was, well, Abuela!"

Isla dug out the Golden Spoon trophy from underneath her pillow. "She didn't win. You guys did!"

A monkey stuck a finger in his ear. "*Us?* Are my monkey's ears tricking me?"

"Abuela is very nice. She wants you guys to have the trophy," Fitz said.

Chef Plum did the unthinkable. He hopped up and gave Isla a big hug.

"I might cry," a toucan whispered.

"The Critter Café welcomes you back ALWAYS," Chef Plum said. "And please, call me Plum."

Isla grinned. There was nothing like a good old Sol Bake Off. Teamwork made everything much more delicious!

DON'T MISS ISLA'S NEXT ADVENTURE!

HERE'S A SNEAK PEEK!

◆◆◆◆◆◆◆◆◆◆◆◆◆◆

Tucked into the corner of the Sol Librería, Isla Verde sat with books scattered on the floor.

She picked up a book titled *Purr-fect Cats* and flipped to a random page filled with fun facts.

"Oooh, listen to this!" Isla said. "This says that cats are *very* wise. What do you think about that?"

Gatito, the cat on her lap, blinked sleepily.

Isla had always thought his name was a bit funny, because Gatito meant "kitten." And he was definitely no longer a kitten.

"I *am* very wise," Gatito purred. "And do you know what else is wise?"

"Let me guess . . . is it doing this?" Isla scratched between his ears.

He purred and snuggled closer. Cats were beings of few words.

For as long as Isla could remember, Gatito had lived in the nature section of the bookstore.

He had a soft bed, a fish-shaped food bowl, and toys hidden around the shelves. If there was a book Isla needed to find, he was the perfect cat for the job.

"Would you mind keeping the purring down, kitty?" Isla's gecko best friend, Fitz, asked. He stood on an open book, focused on a photo of a star fruit tart. "I'm trying to memorize this recipe."

Gatito purred even louder. "Shouldn't you *read* the recipe instead of staring at it?"

"You don't know ingredients like I do," Fitz huffed. "Trust me, I can stare at food and know what's in it."

"Geckos," Gatito muttered.

"Test, test—is this thing on? Oh, yes!" a voice called from the store intercom. "*Ahem*—could Isla Verde please stop by the gift-wrapping station? Thank you."

"Duty calls!" Isla picked up Gatito

and placed him in his bed. "Would you mind stacking these books for me?"

The cat curled his tail around his body. "Only if you take the gecko with you."

Fitz stuck out his hand. "Talk to the sticky gecko feet!"

Isla giggled and placed him on her shoulder. She weaved through the maze of shelves, pushing in any books that stuck out.

Near the front door, Mama and Abuela were placing a bow on an extra-large wrapped present. Each year, they volunteered at the store just in time for the holiday season.